SIMON JAMES

FROG and BEAVER

WITHDRAWN FROM STOCK

WALKER BOOKS

AND SUBSIDIARIES

LONDON • BOSTON • SYDNEY • AUCKLAND

Simon James is an award-winning author and illustrator of books for children and is a regular speaker in schools and at festivals across the UK and the US. His books include *Rex, Nurse Clementine, George Flies South, Dear Greenpeace, Leon and Bob, Sally and the Limpet* and the bestselling Baby Brains series. Simon likes to draw with a dip pen and uses watercolour paints for his illustrations. To find out more about Simon James and his books, visit **www.simonjamesbooks.com**

First published 2017 by Walker Books Ltd
87 Vauxhall Walk, London SE11 5HJ

1 3 5 7 9 10 8 6 4 2

© 2017 Simon James

The right of Simon James to be identified as author/illustrator of this work has been asserted by him
in accordance with the Copyright, Designs and Patents Act 1988

This book has been typeset in Goudy Old Style Educational

Printed in China

British Library Cataloguing in Publication Data:
a catalogue record for this book is available from the British Library

ISBN 978-1-4063-5986-2

www.walker.co.uk

Every morning Frog woke up from under his leaf
and looked out over a beautiful river.

Frog shared the river with his friends: the ducks and their ducklings,
the water voles and their baby water voles.

Everyone lived happily together. It was perfect.

Then one day, a young beaver came swimming down the river.

"Hello, little fella," said the beaver. "I'm Beaver!"

"Hello, Friend," said Frog.

"I'm looking for a place to build my first dam," said Beaver.

"It's going to be the biggest and best dam you've ever seen!"

"Well, this is a great place to live," said Frog. "You'll love it here."

"Wonderful!" said Beaver. "I'll get chewing."

But the next day, Frog woke to see the water in the river was very low.

"What's happened?" said Vole. "We can hardly swim."

"It's that beaver," said Duck. "Have you seen the size of his dam?"

"Leave it to me," said Frog.

"I'll go and see him."

"Hello, Beaver," said Frog. "Can I have a word?"

"Sorry, Frog. Can't stop to chat. Have you seen my dam? Isn't it fantastic?"

"Well, yes," said Frog. "But it's stopping all the water."

Beaver was too excited to listen.

"This is going to be the best dam for miles around," he said.

"Everyone will love it."

The following day the water in the river had almost gone.

"It's that bloomin' beaver," said Duck. "Who does he think he is?"

"I wish I was bigger," said Vole. "I'd teach him a lesson!"

"Oh dear," sighed Frog. "I'll talk to him again."

"Look!" said Beaver, as soon as he saw Frog. "I told you my dam would be the best!"

"But Beaver," said Frog, "why does it have to be so big? We haven't any water left."

"There's lots of water on my side," said Beaver. "Why don't you all move up here?"

"Why do *we* have to move upstream?" groaned Duck.

"I'm sorry," said Frog. "Beaver just wouldn't listen."

"I wish I was bigger," muttered Vole. "I'd tell him where to go."

When they arrived, Frog introduced everyone to Beaver.

"Hello," said Beaver. "Look at my dam, isn't it amazing?"

"Humph," muttered Duck.

That evening, Frog helped the
ducks collect sticks to build
a nest for the night.

Then he helped the water
voles dig a new hole.

Finally, Frog fell asleep
under an old leaf.

By morning, Beaver had finished his enormous dam.

"It's brilliant," boasted Beaver. "It's nearly as tall as the mountains!"

"Frog! Frog! Look! It's the best dam in the whole world!"

Frog looked. He saw the huge dam, but he also saw the water about to burst over the top. "Look out Beaver!" shouted Frog.

Suddenly, branches began
to creak and snap.

Stones tumbled!
Boulders crashed!

And then …

whoosh!

The water came crashing through the dam. Beaver was sent tumbling over and over again as boulders and branches sped by.

And then came the ducks and the ducklings,
the water voles and the baby water voles and, of course, Frog.
"Swim for the bank!" shouted Frog.

The ducks, the water voles and Frog all made it safely to the shore.

"Is everybody okay?" asked Frog.

"We're okay," said Vole, "but I think Beaver's in trouble…"

"Is he all right?" asked Duck.

"He's swallowed too much water," said Frog,

"but I know what to do."

Frog jumped up and down on Beaver's back until Beaver began to cough and splutter.

"W-where am I? What happened?" asked Beaver.
"Your dam burst," said Duck.
"Frog saved your life."

Beaver was quiet for a moment. "How can I ever thank you, Frog?" he gasped.

"Well, we've lost our homes again," sighed Frog. "Perhaps you could help?"

"Anything!" said Beaver eagerly.

So Beaver helped the ducks build a new nest.
"Not too big though," said Duck.

And he dug a new hole for the water voles and the baby water voles.
"Not too big though," said Vole.

And finally, Beaver built a dam for himself – not too big though.

Everything on the river was perfect again ...

especially for Beaver's best friend, Frog.